[SURVIVING THE IMPOSSIBLE]

SURVIVING
A ROBOT
REVOLUTION

CHARLIE OGDEN

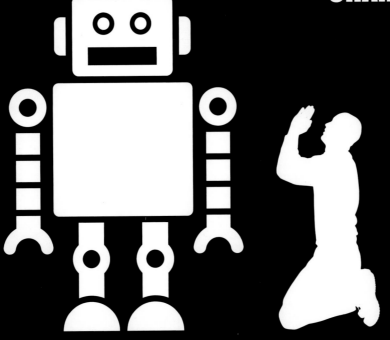

Gareth Stevens
PUBLISHING

Please visit our website, **www.garethstevens.com**.
For a free color catalog of all our high-quality books,
call toll free 1-800-542-2595 or fax 1-877-542-2596.

CATALOGING-IN-PUBLICATION DATA

Names: Ogden, Charlie.
Title: Surviving a robot revolution / Charlie Ogden.
Description: New York : Gareth Stevens Publishing, 2018. | Series: Surviving the impossible | Includes index.
Identifiers: ISBN 9781538214596 (pbk.) | ISBN 9781538214206 (library bound) | ISBN 9781538214602 (6 pack)
Subjects: LCSH: Artificial intelligence--Juvenile literature. | Disasters--Juvenile literature. | Survival--Juvenile literature.
Classification: LCC Q335.4 O43 2018 | DDC 006.3--dc23

Published in 2018 by
Gareth Stevens Publishing
11 East 14th Street, Suite 349
New York, NY 10003

Written by: Charlie Ogden
Edited by: Kirsty Holmes
Designed by: Danielle Jones

Photocredits: Abbreviations: l–left, r–right, b–bottom, t–top, c–centre, m–middle. Images are courtesy of Shutterstock.com. With thanks to Getty Images, Thinkstock Photo and iStockphoto. Front cover – tr & bl – By Zhee–Shee, bg – ilolab, Jesus Robert. 1 – DarkGeometrysStudios. 4– Ociacia . 5bg –Roberts Photography, 5l – Chiradech Chotchuang , 5c – DJTaylor. 6t – maxuser, 6b – Christian Lagerek. 7 – DarkGeometryStudios. 8 – Digital Storm. 9bg – Semisatch, 9c – SvedOliver, 9b –Ljupco Smokovski. 10 – Khamidulin Sergey. 11 – breakermaximus. 12tr – Shevs, 12l – XiXinXing, 12b – Guillermo del Olmo. 13tl – Ociacia 13br –VaLiza. 14t – Vlue, 14bl – Flas100, 14l – Dagmara_K , 14bc – Axel Bueckert. 15t – Mr.Yodchai Promduang, 15c – tinka's. 16m – 135pixels. 17r – twomeerkats, 18m – Photographee, 19m – taewafeel, 20m – Phonlamai Photo, t&b – STILLFX. 21 – Tatiana Shepeleva. 22bg – Gennady Grechishkin, br – Dario Lo Presti. 23 – stockchairatgfx, 23br – Josh McCann. 24 – volodyar. 25 – Willyam Bradberry. 26bg – Ae Cherayut, t – ILeysen, – tsuneomp. 27 – Sicco Hesselmans. 28bg – blvdone. 29bg – blvdone, br – F.Schmidt. 30bg leoks.

Printed in China

CPSIA compliance information: Batch CW18GS: For further information contact
Gareth Stevens, New York, New York at 1-800-542-2595.

CONTENTS

Words that look like THIS can be found in the glossary on page 31.

ROBOTS

Everyone's watched a robot movie or two, and the story is nearly always the same – humans create robots that turn against their creators and attempt to destroy the whole human RACE. When killer robots are on the loose, we humans normally find some way of beating them, and planet Earth returns to normal once more. But if there really was a robot REVOLUTION, it might not be that easy. Would we really be able to overcome stronger, smarter mechanical versions of ourselves?

THE ROBOT ARMY

There are around 8.6 million robots in the world today and that number is growing by around 25% every single year. A robot is a machine that is able to follow complicated instructions AUTOMATICALLY. Robots are controlled by a computer. They can be small machines helping to build things in factories or super-intelligent, humanlike machines. Using robots to help us seems to make perfect sense. After all, robots don't get sick or tired like humans do.

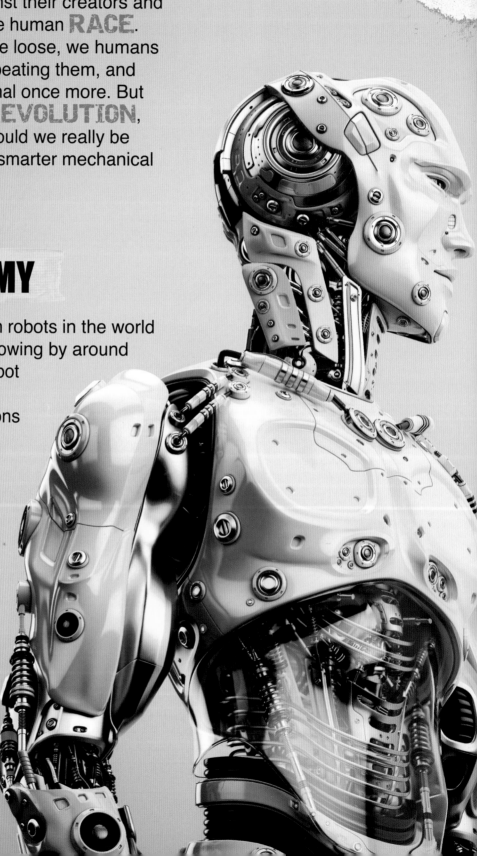

4

THE ROBOT TAKEOVER

Robot experts predict that in less than 30 years, the number of robots on the planet will be more than the number of humans. That means we'll have billions of super-intelligent robots working in our stores, building things in our factories, and maybe even helping in our homes picking up our smelly socks for us! If we made them work this hard, would they turn against us and destroy us? What would the world look like with robots in charge?

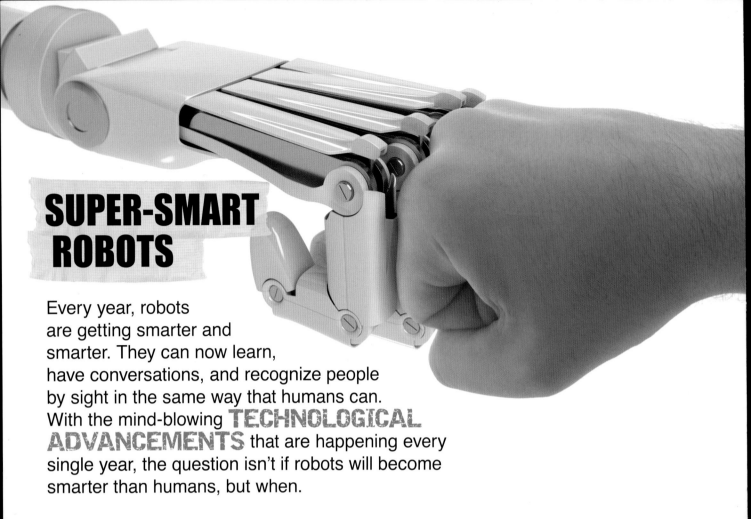

SUPER-SMART ROBOTS

Every year, robots are getting smarter and smarter. They can now learn, have conversations, and recognize people by sight in the same way that humans can. With the mind-blowing TECHNOLOGICAL ADVANCEMENTS that are happening every single year, the question isn't if robots will become smarter than humans, but when.

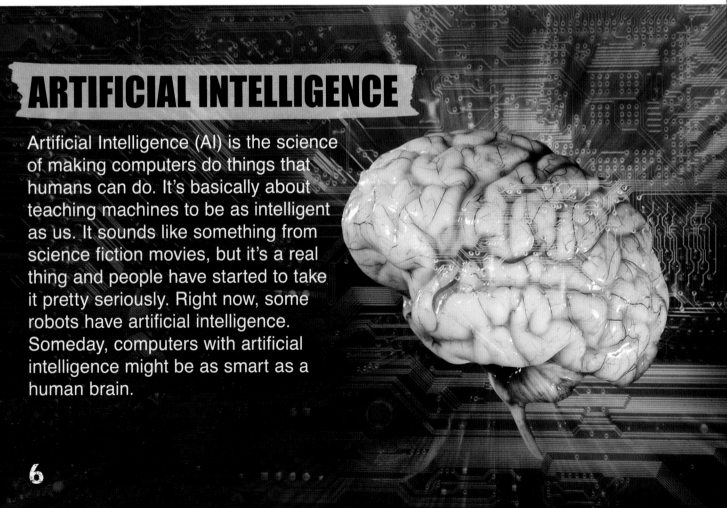

ARTIFICIAL INTELLIGENCE

Artificial Intelligence (AI) is the science of making computers do things that humans can do. It's basically about teaching machines to be as intelligent as us. It sounds like something from science fiction movies, but it's a real thing and people have started to take it pretty seriously. Right now, some robots have artificial intelligence. Someday, computers with artificial intelligence might be as smart as a human brain.

ARTIFICIAL SUPER-INTELLIGENCE

If AI sounds scary, things are about to get a whole lot scarier! People all around the world are terrified of what will happen when robots have Artificial Super-intelligence (ASI). Robots with ASI would be much smarter than even the most intelligent human being in every possible way. Recent technological advancements mean that a world where robots have Artificial Super-intelligence (ASI) is a very real possibility. When computers have ASI, a robot revolution could be just around the corner.

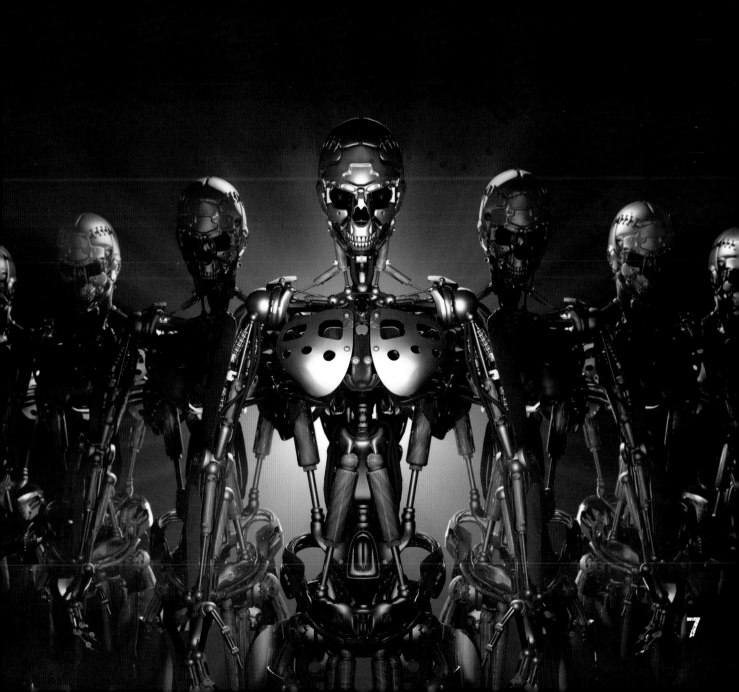

IF ROBOTS RULED THE WORLD...

There's no way to know exactly what ASI will do, or what the consequences of creating these brainy-bots will be for us. It's possible ASI would be kind and peaceful! But we do know that with intelligence comes power. We know this because, at the moment, we're at the top of the world. Humans are the most intelligent SPECIES on the planet. We can read, write, and talk – we've even invented things like planes and spaceships. Because of this, we've DOMINATED life on Earth for thousands of years.

GOOD VS. EVIL

We have no idea whether ASI robots will be helpful or harmful. We could live peacefully together as friendly neighbors, or robots might try to take over the world and destroy the human race. While we don't know what a bunch of super-smart robots might mean for our lives or our futures, we do know that if the worst does happen and we're faced with a robot revolution, then we're going to need to be ready for it.

ROBOT REVOLUTION

Imagine that you're watching your favorite TV show when suddenly, the picture begins to crackle, the theme song dies away, and a robot head appears on the screen. Its eyes are fiery red, and it's shouting something in a metallic voice: "Beware the revolution!"

Soon you realize they've taken over the GOVERNMENT and are trying to destroy every human on the planet! The robot revolution is happening, and to survive it, you're going to need to be smart! Really smart. So keep your cool, and most importantly, try to stay alive.

A SAFE PLACE TO HIDE

It might be a while before you find out about the revolution. These super-smart robots are likely to wait patiently for the perfect time to begin their takeover. Whenever you find out, you need to be prepared.

What's the first thing that you do if a bunch of killer robots is heading your way? Find a safe place to hide of course! This will buy you some time so you can work out how to fight back. Don't let them spot you on the way to your hideout. When you've picked a hideout, keep it secret – you can't trust anyone now that there are

Try to head towards the countryside and avoid large towns and cities if possible. It's likely that the robots will be focusing on the places where they can destroy the most humans. Once you get to a hideout, it's important not to stay there too long. Get organized, and then move on. Eventually, they'll figure out where you are and come looking for you!

HOW TO SPOT A ROBOT

IN THE SAME SKIN

You might think that spotting a robot would be easy. Their metal bodies would be the first big giveaway along with their strange computerized voices and awkward robotic walk. You'll know for sure when you're in the presence of a robot, right? Think again! They might just look exactly like us. If they're smarter than us and they want to take over the world, they might have developed the technology to completely disguise themselves as humans. Could your friends, family members, and teachers secretly be robots in disguise, ready to stage their takeover? How can you tell if you're dealing with a killer robot or a normal human?

When the robots take over, you might have only seconds to figure out if someone's a human or a killer robot trying to destroy you. Learning how to spot a robot is one of the most important things that you'll need to know if you're going to survive the robot revolution.

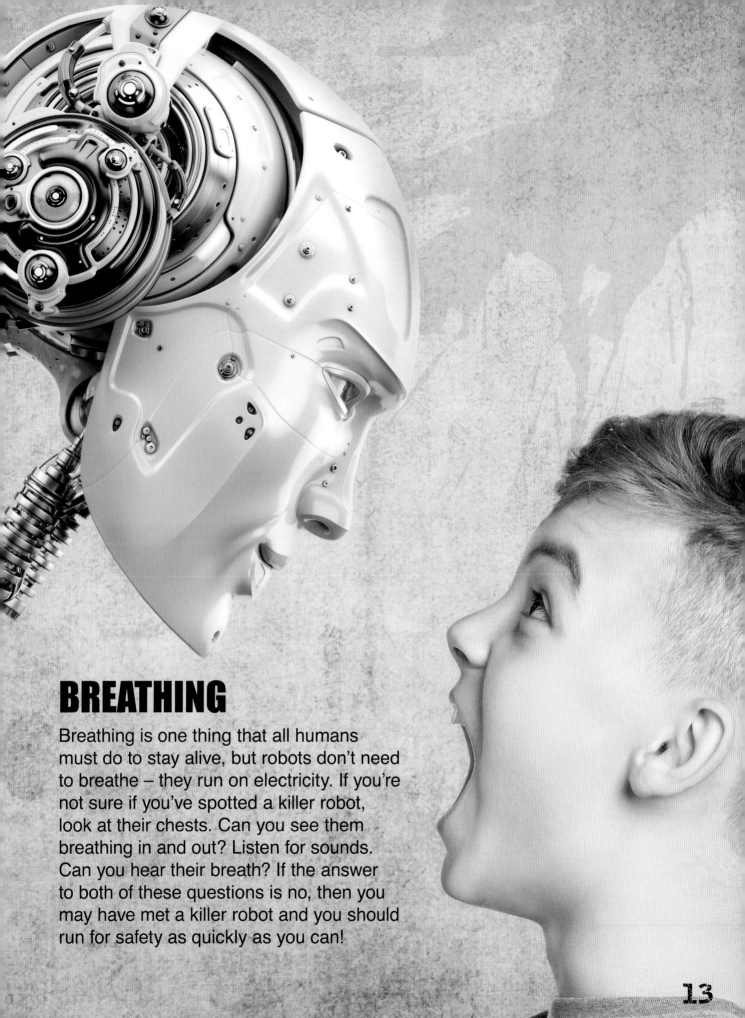

BREATHING

Breathing is one thing that all humans must do to stay alive, but robots don't need to breathe – they run on electricity. If you're not sure if you've spotted a killer robot, look at their chests. Can you see them breathing in and out? Listen for sounds. Can you hear their breath? If the answer to both of these questions is no, then you may have met a killer robot and you should run for safety as quickly as you can!

SPOT THE SIGNS

Just like breathing, robots don't need to sleep, eat, or do other basic human things like going to the bathroom or taking a shower. Watch out for people who don't like snacks, are always awake, never break a sweat, and never excuse themselves to go to the bathroom. All of these are signs that a robot has **INFILTRATED** your group of friends and you could be seconds away from total **ANNIHILATION**!

PAIN

Robots can't feel pain. If you see someone step on a sharp object or bump into a wall without reacting, they might be a robot in disguise. Robots can't bleed, either. If a robot got a cut, you'd probably see metal under their skin instead of blood!

You should never try to hurt someone to test if they're a robot. If they're not, then you might seriously injure a fellow human. However, if you notice someone who never seems to feel pain, they just might be a killer robot.

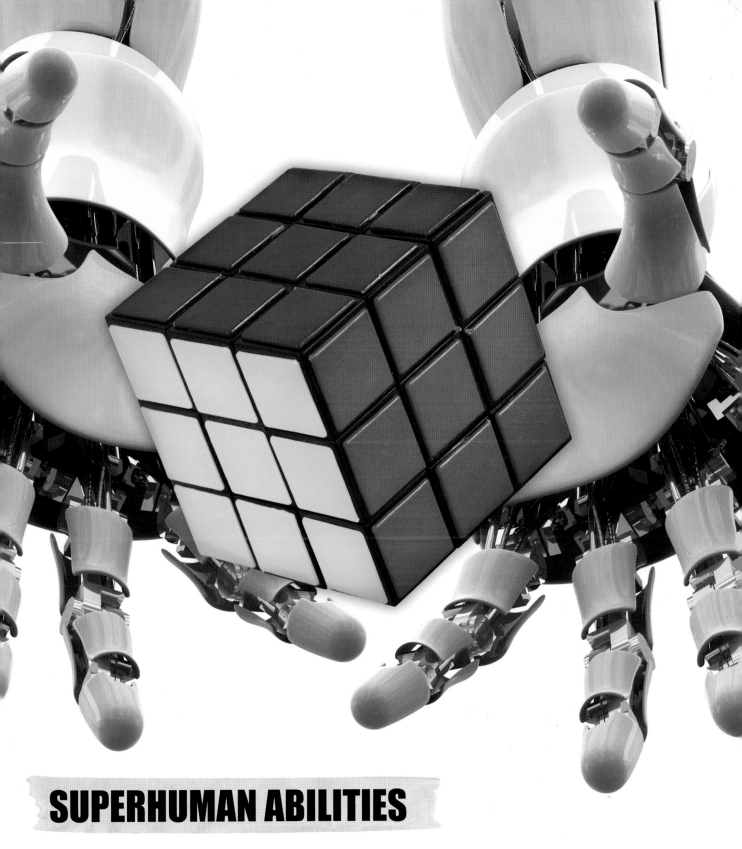

SUPERHUMAN ABILITIES

Remember, these robots are smarter than us in every single way, so you need to look out for their superhuman abilities. These are the clearest signs that you're in the presence of a robot.

If your friend is the best in math class, can solve a Rubik's Cube in less than a second, or beat your whole group at chess in minutes, then you might be in the presence of a robot with superhuman abilities.

BEING HUMAN

Some of the many advantages of being a super-intelligent killer robot are that you don't need to eat food, drink water, sleep, or breathe to stay alive. Robots will be well aware of this advantage and might try to use your human weakness against you.

They could destroy everything that's essential to your survival – food supplies, medicines, drinking water, and a whole lot more. These are the things that you're going to have to find if you're going to have any chance of toughing this out.

FOOD AND WATER

Unless a killer robot is right outside your door, you'll have time to take as much food and water as you can carry from your home to your hideout. Make sure you know where the nearest grocery stores and natural water sources are in relation to your hideout.

You're going to have to go out at some point and find more supplies, but knowing how to get there could give you a head start that might just save your life.

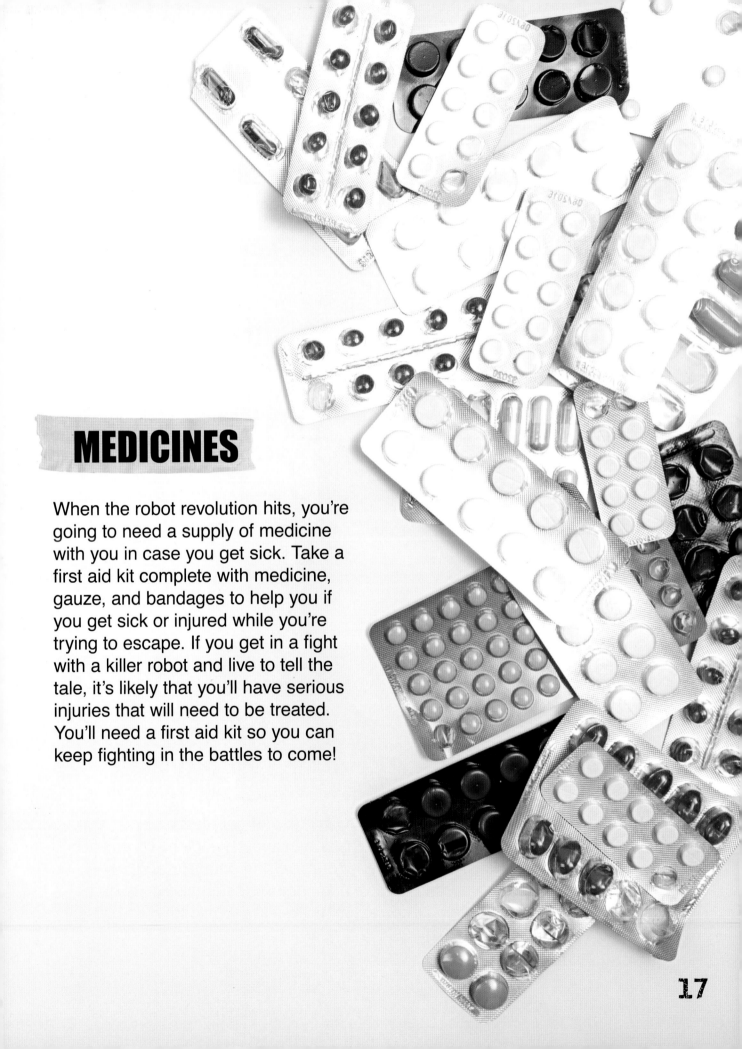

MEDICINES

When the robot revolution hits, you're going to need a supply of medicine with you in case you get sick. Take a first aid kit complete with medicine, gauze, and bandages to help you if you get sick or injured while you're trying to escape. If you get in a fight with a killer robot and live to tell the tale, it's likely that you'll have serious injuries that will need to be treated. You'll need a first aid kit so you can keep fighting in the battles to come!

WORKING TOGETHER

When the first group of robots take over the world, it's highly likely that there will be any number of robot wars over who gets to be in charge of the human slaves. Different groups of robots might turn against each other and try to gain total power. Make the most of this chaos. It will give you the time that you need to gather people and plan your **RESISTANCE**.

EXPERTS

To outsmart these super-intelligent bots, you're going to have to pool the smartest brains together to figure out how to survive. Robot experts or computer programmers should be your first priority. Finding people who know how the robots work might just be the key to destroying them.

Other useful people to have in your group include a doctor to help you when anyone gets injured and an engineer to design and build new machines that could help you defeat the robots.

PURE EVIL?

Not all robots will be trying to destroy you. Robots were first made to help humans, and some will still be PROGRAMMED to do this. These helpful robots might try to join your group. You should let them use their superintelligence to help you plan your victory over the killer robots. But remember – don't trust everyone who walks through your door. Figure out if they are killer robots in disguise or friendly robots, key to your future survival.

VHF/UHF FM TRANSCEIVER

CLR F
1 SQL 2 VOX 3 REV # V/M
4 STEP 5 DUP 6 SCN 0
7 R.T 8 T.T 9 SET * ⟲

IC-092

Top Tip: Make sure you have ways to communicate with other members of your group if you become split up. Walkie-talkies, radios, or even whistles might be useful when you get in trouble.

KNOW THEIR WEAKNESSES

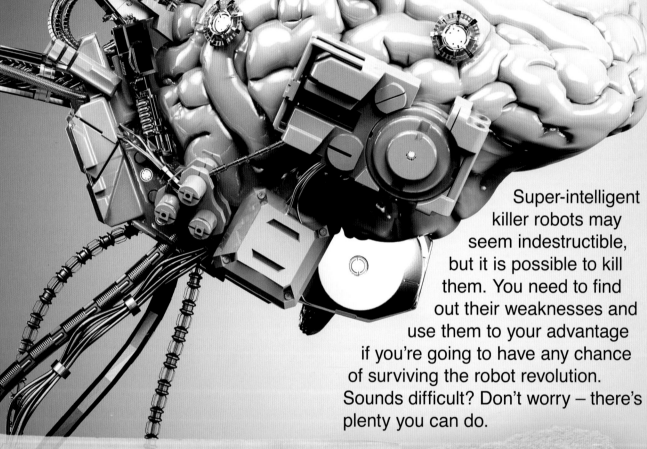

Super-intelligent killer robots may seem indestructible, but it is possible to kill them. You need to find out their weaknesses and use them to your advantage if you're going to have any chance of surviving the robot revolution. Sounds difficult? Don't worry – there's plenty you can do.

NOT THE SHARPEST KNIFE IN THE DRAWER

These robots might have "super-intelligence," but they will probably have different strengths, just like humans. They might be able to solve the world's longest math equation, but their senses probably won't be as sharp as ours.

They might not be able to see, hear, or feel as well as us, which might make them easier to sneak up on. With this in mind, go after the weakest or least intelligent robots first. They will be the easiest targets. Once this is done,

FOREVER LEARNING

But remember, because these robots are smart, they'll learn to **ADAPT** to human attacks by developing new defenses. As soon as you've started to find out their weaknesses, be on the lookout for new robot technology. They've never been attacked before, so at first, they'll probably be unprepared for what you're about to throw at them. But they'll quickly learn to outsmart you again.

HOW TO FIGHT A ROBOT

You've found a hideout, escaped robot capture, gathered a resistance group, and studied robot weaknesses. Now you're going to need to know how to fight the robots when they come for you. If you follow this guide, you might just make it out of here alive.

WEAPONS

Weapons are very important for surviving the robot revolution. You're going to need to be able to defend yourself against any surprise attacks or robot AMBUSHES that may result in sudden death. Weapons are only good for defending yourself against physical attacks, but they might just keep you alive long enough to run away.

ALL BRAIN NO BRAWN

By now you know there's no way to outsmart a robot that has ASI, but don't lose hope. There's something important to remember about robots – they run on computers. The computer is like the robot's brain. It controls all the bot's actions, including its violent ones. Once you've destroyed the computer, you've destroyed the robot. Instead of focusing on trying to fight the bots, you need to get their computers. You'll need some special skills, but it can be done.

Top Tip: While it might seem like a good idea to shoot robots, it is not. Robots are made of metal and do not feel bullets like humans do.

OVERRIDE THE COMPUTER

Killer robots were originally programmed to help us out, but somewhere along the line, their systems malfunctioned and their sole purpose became the destruction of humanity. However, because they were programmed in the first place, they can be reprogrammed.

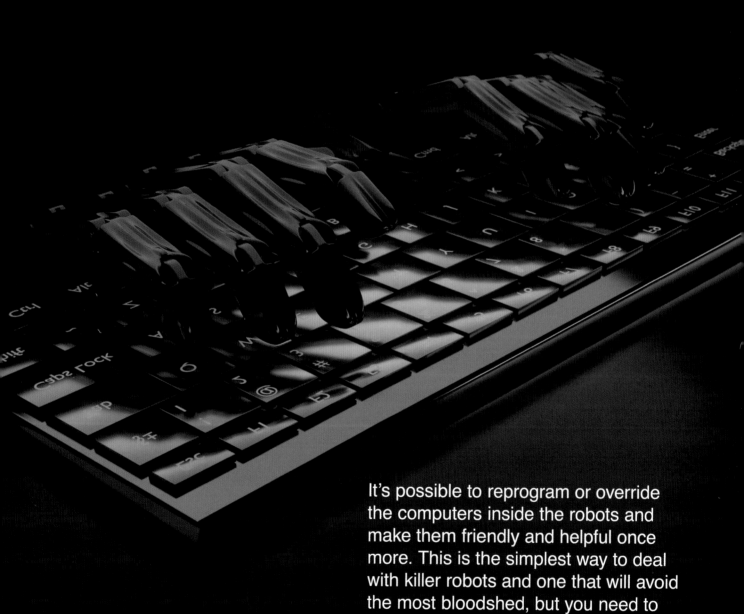

It's possible to reprogram or override the computers inside the robots and make them friendly and helpful once more. This is the simplest way to deal with killer robots and one that will avoid the most bloodshed, but you need to make sure you've got the right people on your team who know what they are doing. Otherwise, things could get much worse for you!

BUILDING A BETTER ROBOT

Your other option is to build a new, more intelligent army of robots programmed to defeat the killer ones. If you do choose to do this, be very careful. You could end up creating a super-super-intelligent new army of super-killer robots, and you've got enough on your plate already. If this goes wrong, you will have doomed the entire world, and you won't survive that.

THE HELPFUL ROBOT ARMY

If you have been lucky enough to find some robots that are still programmed to be friendly, hang on to them. They can infiltrate the killer robot army. By pretending to be one of the killer robots, your helpful robot could gain important information and report back to you. They can protect you while you find a way to override the killer robots' computers.

HAVE YOU GOT THE METAL?

We already know that to destroy a killer robot, you need to reprogram its computer. However, when there is a thick layer of metal protecting that computer, it can be difficult to reach. You might be able to melt the killer robots down by taking them to a **SMELTER** and applying some serious heat to their metal bodies. You could also try to find materials that will **CORRODE** their metal bodies. Depending on what metal they're made from, you could use a number of materials, such an acid, to seriously weaken or destroy your killer enemies.

WATER

Once you've corroded their bodies, you'll be able to make the final blow to their computers. Computers run on electricity – but what trumps electricity? That's right. Water! You will need to use a water attack on the bots. Their computers are likely to **SHORT CIRCUIT** in water. Find as many **HYDRANTS**, hoses, and water guns as possible. When they get close, blast them into oblivion with a flood of water.

EMP DEVICE

Another way to defeat the robot army would be by using an electromagnetic pulse (EMP) device. This is a piece of technology that can destroy all electronic devices, including phones, computers, and even robots. It does this by sending out a blast of magnetic energy. However, it is important to only use this as a last resort. It will destroy the robots but it will destroy all other computers and electronic equipment too. There will be no electricity, and then you'll have a whole new challenge on your hands: surviving in a world without power.

LIVING IN PERFECT HARMONY

If you've survived the robot revolution, you're going to have to learn to live alongside robots in perfect harmony. Some robots are good, and they can help you with their super-smart brains. So don't destroy them all – make peace with the friendly bots. The road to perfect robot-human relations is not going to be easy, but you'll get there, eventually.

KEEPING THE PEACE

To prevent another robot revolution from taking place, perhaps you should ask the robots why they turned against you in the first place. Maybe they were sick of picking up our dirty socks or doing all our math homework without getting any praise. Robots have feelings too, you know!

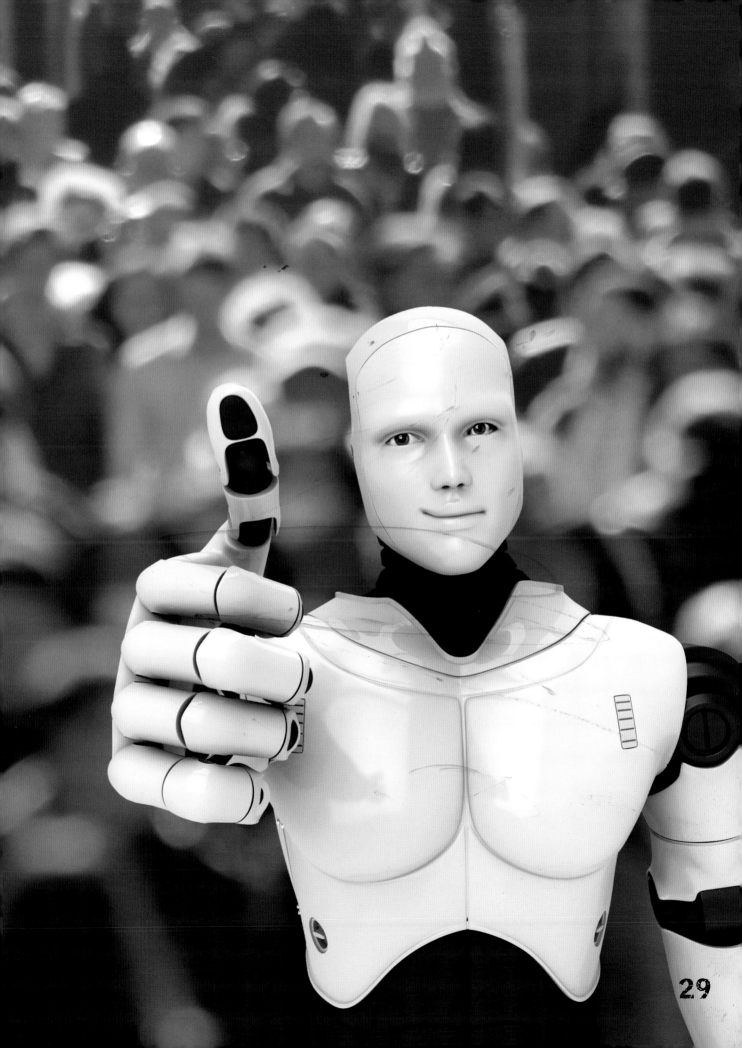

SURVIVING THE ROBOT REVOLUTION

If you follow this guide, then you might just make it through the robot revolution. You've learned how to find a decent hideout, gather supplies, and spot a killer robot in disguise. You also know the killer robots' weaknesses. If you have to fight one, you now know how to protect yourself and stay alive.

If you manage to survive the impossible, then take it easy for a while. Enjoy the good life, take a vacation on an island, and focus on doing the things that you love, safe in the knowledge that if killer robots strike again, you'll know what to do.

GLOSSARY

ADAPT	change over time to suit different conditions
AMBUSHES	surprise attacks by people or robots who are hiding
ANNIHILATION	total destruction
AUTOMATICALLY	without conscious thought or control
CORRODE	destroy or damage over time through a chemical reaction
DOMINATED	ruled over or controlled
GOVERNMENT	the group of people with the authority to run a country and decide its laws
HYDRANTS	upright pipes with nozzles used for getting water from a main pipe
INFILTRATED	to have moved into an organization or country secretly, without being detected
PROGRAMMED	to have developed a set of instructions to allow computers to do certain things
RACE	a group of people who share the same culture, history, or ethnicity
RESISTANCE	the act of resisting or opposing someone or something
REVOLUTION	to overthrow a government or system, often accompanied with violence
SHORT CIRCUIT	the failure of electricity to flow properly because the wires or connections in the circuit are damaged
SMELTER	a factory or workplace used to melt iron
SPECIES	a group of very similar animals or plants that are capable of producing young together
TECHNOLOGICAL ADVANCEMENTS	relating to improvements in technology

INDEX